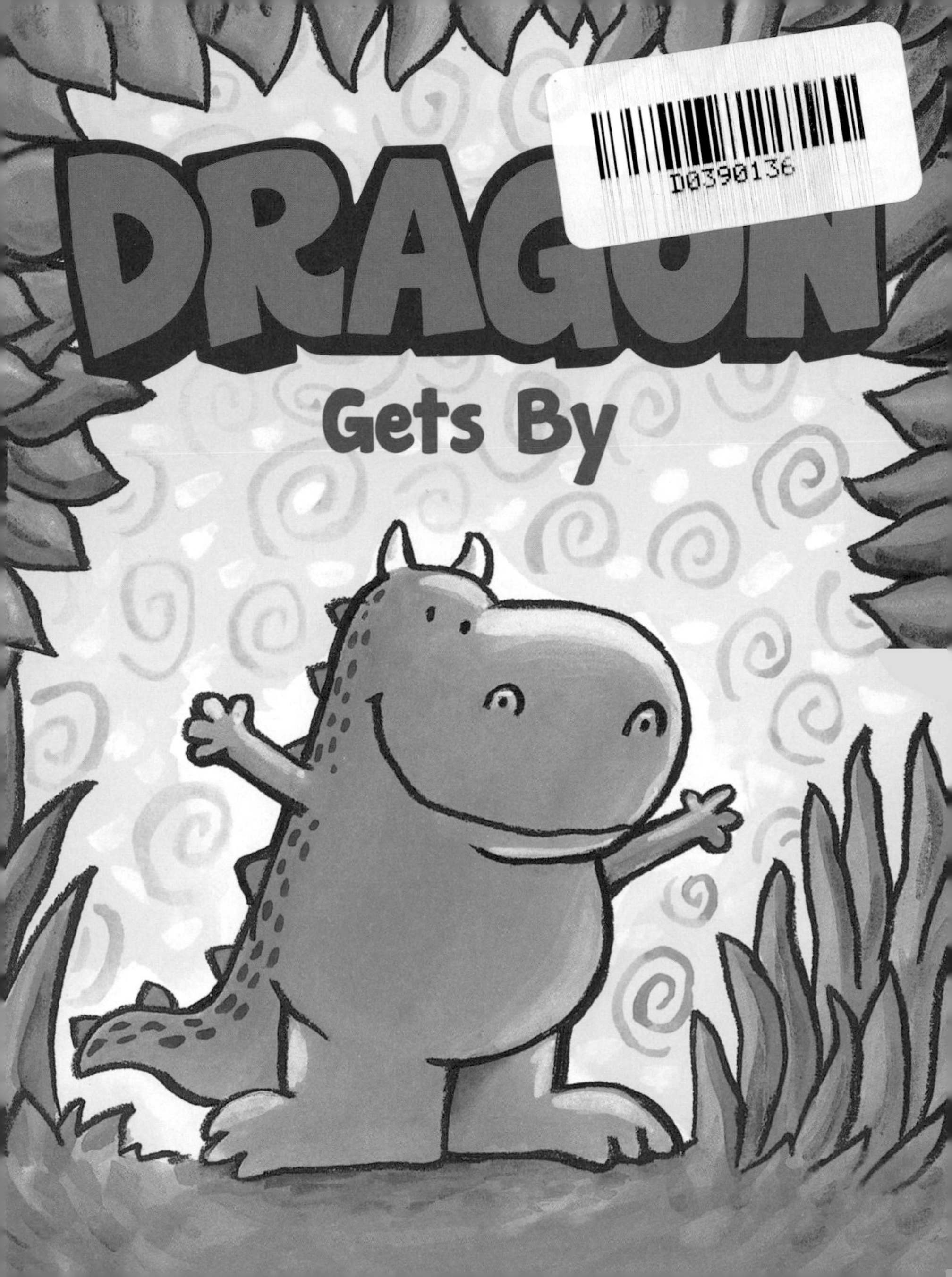
DRAGON
Gets By

Read the complete DRAGON series!

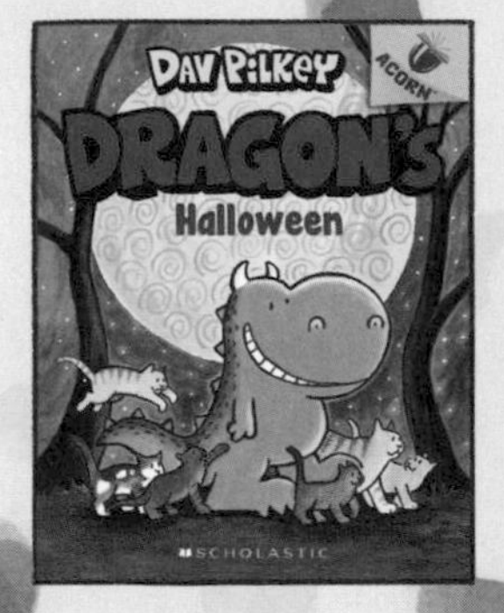

DRAGON

Gets By

DAV PILKEY

ACORN™
SCHOLASTIC INC.

For my old pal George Hurst

Library of Congress Cataloging-in-Publication Data

Names: Pilkey, Dav, 1966– author, illustrator.
Title: Dragon gets by / Dav Pilkey.
Description: New York : Acorn/Scholastic Inc., 2020. | Series: Dragon ; 3 | Originally published: New York : Orchard Books, 1991. | Summary: Whenever Dragon wakes up groggy, he always does everything wrong, like sweeping a hole in his dirt floor, or reading an egg and frying his newspaper.
Identifiers: LCCN 2018046398| ISBN 9781338347517 (hc : alk. paper) | ISBN 9781338347500 (pb : alk. paper)
Subjects: LCSH: Dragons — Juvenile fiction. | Chores — Juvenile fiction. | Humorous stories. | CYAC: Dragons — Fiction. | Chores — Fiction. | Humorous stories. | LCGFT: Humorous fiction. | Picture books.
Classification: LCC PZ7.P63123 Dr 2020 | DDC [E] — dc23
LC record available at https://lccn.loc.gov/2018046398

10 9 8 7 6 5 4 3 2 20 21 22 23 24

Printed in China 62
This edition first printing, January 2020
Book design by Dav Pilkey and Sarah Dvojack

Contents

1
Dragon Sees the Day

One warm, sunny morning
Dragon woke up and yawned.
He was very groggy . . .
And whenever Dragon woke up groggy,
he did **everything** wrong.

First, he read an egg
and fried the morning newspaper.

Then he buttered his tea
and sipped a cup of toast.

Finally, Dragon opened the door
to see the day.
But Dragon did not see the sun.
He did not see the trees or the hills
or the flowers or the sky.
He saw only shadows.

"It must still be nighttime,"
said Dragon.

So he went back to bed.

2
Housework

Dragon's floor was very dirty.
He got his broom and began to sweep.

When he was finished sweeping,
the floor was still dirty.

So Dragon swept again . . .
And there was still dirt everywhere.

"There sure is a lot of dirt
on this floor," said Dragon.

Dragon swept all morning long,
and into the afternoon.
He carried out wheelbarrows
filled with dirt.

All of his sweeping left
a very big hole in his floor.

Finally, the mailmouse came by.
She looked at all the dirt
outside the house.

She looked at the big hole
inside the house.

"What's going on in here?"
asked the mailmouse.

"I'm sweeping my floor," said Dragon.
"It is very dirty."

"But you have a dirt floor,"
said the mailmouse.
"It is made of dirt."

Dragon looked at the hole he had swept, and scratched his big head.

"Looks like you've made a mess," said the mailmouse.

"Looks like I've made a basement," said Dragon.

3
Yardwork

Dragon looked at the big pile of dirt
in his yard.
"What am I going to do with all this dirt?"
he wondered.

He got a shovel
and dug a big, deep hole.

Then he scooped the dirt into the hole.

"Well, that takes care of that,"
said Dragon.

"Now where did **this** come from?"

4
Shopping

Dragon looked in his cupboard,
but there was no food at all.

"The cupboard is bare," said Dragon.
"Time to go shopping."

Dragon got into his car and drove.
The food store was at the top of a hill.
It was a very steep drive.

Dragon loved to go shopping.
He was a very wise shopper.
He bought food only from
the five basic food groups:

He bought cheese curls
from the dairy group.
He bought doughnuts
from the bread group.

He bought catsup
from the fruits and vegetables group.
He bought pork rinds
from the meat group.

FUDGE POPS
PORK RINDS
PORK
CATSUP
DOUGHNUTS
CHEESE
DOUGHNUTS

And he bought fudge pops
from the chocolate group.

Dragon had a balanced diet.

He had so much food that he could not fit it all into his car.

"I know what I will do," said Dragon. "I will eat some of the food now, and then the rest will fit in the car."

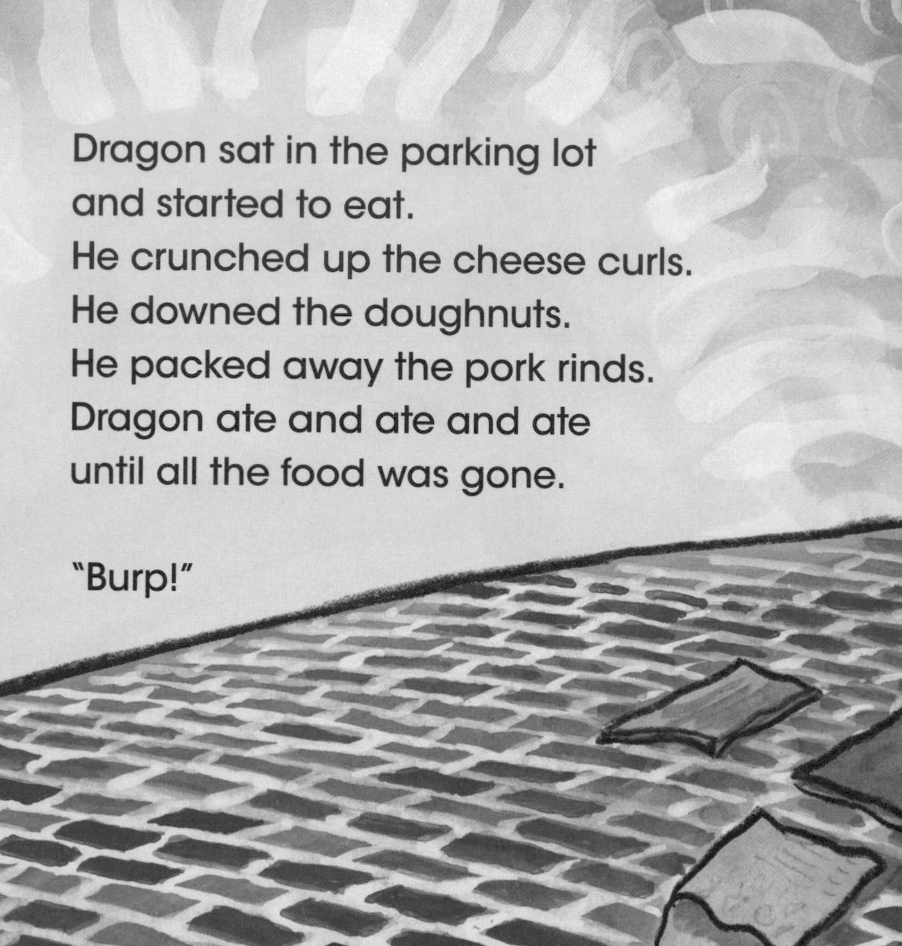

Dragon sat in the parking lot
and started to eat.
He crunched up the cheese curls.
He downed the doughnuts.
He packed away the pork rinds.
Dragon ate and ate and ate
until all the food was gone.

"Burp!"

FUDGE POPS

Now **Dragon** could not fit into his car.

"Oh, what am I going to do?"
cried Dragon.

He thought and thought,
and scratched his big head.

"I know what I will do," said Dragon.
"I will push my car home."

So Dragon pushed his car down the hill.

The car began to roll faster and faster . . .

. . . and faster . . .

. . . and faster.

Finally, Dragon's car came to a stop right in front of his house.

All the excitement had made Dragon
very hungry.
He went into his kitchen
and looked in the cupboard.
There was no food at all.

"The cupboard is bare," said Dragon.
"Time to go shopping."

5
Good Night, Dragon

It had been a long, busy day,
and now it was bedtime.

Dragon was very groggy.
So he brushed his head
and combed his teeth . . .

He watered his bed . . .

. . . crawled into his plants . . .

. . . and fell fast asleep.

About the Author

DAV PILKEY is the creator of the bestselling Dog Man and Captain Underpants series. He has written and illustrated many other books for young readers, including the Caldecott Honor book *The Paperboy*, *Dog Breath*, and *The Hallo-Wiener*. Dav lives in the Pacific Northwest with his wife.

YOU CAN DRAW DRAGON!

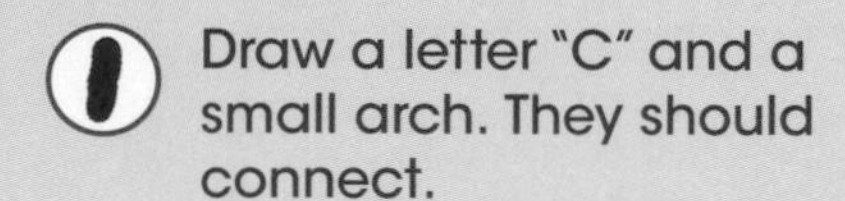

1. Draw a letter "C" and a small arch. They should connect.

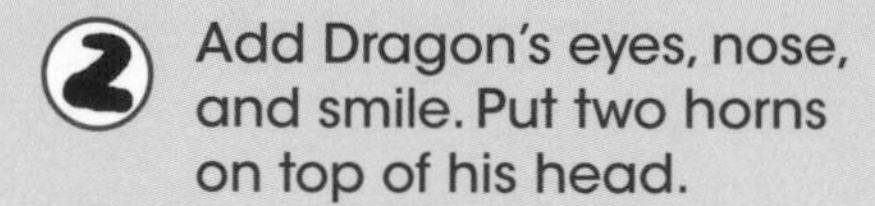

2. Add Dragon's eyes, nose, and smile. Put two horns on top of his head.

3. Draw Dragon's back and tail.

4. Add Dragon's tummy and one of his feet.

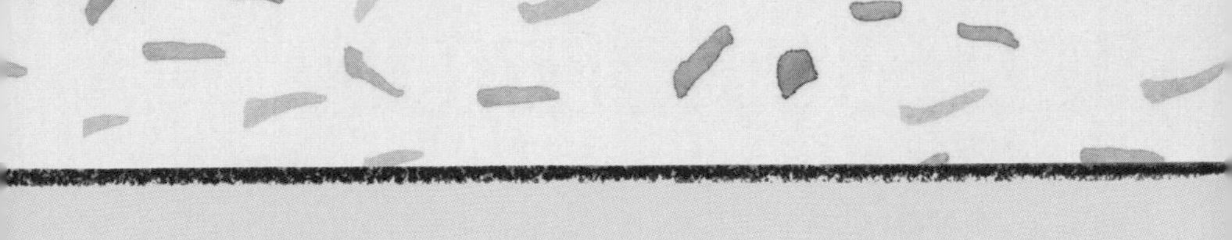

5. Draw Dragon's arms and hands. Don't forget to add his other foot!

6. Draw spikes down his back and on his tail.

7. Add a flower and some grass. Dragon is sniffing the flower!

8. Color in your drawing!

WHAT'S YOUR STORY?

Dragon makes a lot of mistakes when he is groggy.
Imagine **you** did not get enough sleep last night.
What mistakes would you make?
Where would you take a nap?
Write and draw your story!

BONUS!

Try making your story just like Dav — with watercolors! Did you know that Dav taught himself how to watercolor when he was making the Dragon books? He went to the supermarket, bought a children's watercolor set, and used it to paint the entire book series.